MW00909552

A Missing Curiosity

You're Invited!

Visit www.amissingcuriosity.com for
more fun with Mortimer & Parker!

Get your free coloring pages
and much more at
www.amissingcuriosity.com.

A Missing Curiosity

story
Kari M. Kron

art
Illustration Pal

Text copyright @2016 by Kari M. Kron
Illustrations copyright @ 2016 by Illustration Pal
Cover, design and graphic realization by Kari M. Kron

First printing November 2016

All rights reserved.
No part of this publication may be reproduced, stored in a retrieval system
or transmitted in any form or by any means, electronic, mechanical, photocopying,
recording or otherwise without written permission of the publisher.

For information regarding permission, write to KMK Publishing,
Attention: Permissions Department, PO Box 63, Norwich, NY 13815.

Library of Congress Control Number: 2016918173
ebook ISBN 978-1-63451-021-9
paperback ISBN 978-1-63451-022-6
audio book ISBN 978-1-63451-024-0

Printed in USA

Distributed in USA by
KMK Publishing
PO Box 63
Norwich, NY 13815

For
Mom & Dad

One morning Mortimer Mouse is walking along the riverbank to his favorite spot. He likes to munch on the yummy wildflower seeds he finds along the way. When he reaches the bend in the river, he knows he is close. It feels good to take a little time every day to stop and think. What better place to do it than sitting in his tree by the river?

"Do rivers stop and think?" Mortimer wonders to himself as his tree comes into view. He doesn't have time to answer himself, however, because there is already someone in his comfy clearing, sitting on the exposed roots of the tall oak tree.

Mortimer stands on his hind legs and sniffs the air, whiskers twitching. He doesn't recognize the stranger by his smell, though.

"Well, I shouldn't be surprised that someone else is here," Mortimer says to himself. "This is an excellent thinking spot. Just the kind of place to stop and wonder about life, the world, and everything. Perhaps we shall have to keep an appointment book in a box to avoid interruptions."

The visitor stands up and circles behind the tree. Now Mortimer can see the quills sticking up in all directions from the creature's back. "A porcupine! Fascinating, indeed! I wonder why he is here pacing around the tree?"

The porcupine emerges from behind the tree and sighs. He stands up on his hind legs and sniffs the air, his quills reaching out in every direction. After a moment, he plops back down on all fours, quills collapsing, and smells the ground. Then he proceeds to go around the tree again, this time in the opposite direction.

Mortimer sighs, too. "Not only have I found a porcupine, but he doesn't seem to be a very happy porcupine. Perhaps I shall have to find another place to sit and think today. One can hardly sit and think while an upset porcupine is pacing about."

Mortimer decides to continue past the tree along the river to search for another thinking spot. He is almost to the tall grass on the other side of the clearing when a deep voice rumbles, "Hey, you there, little mouse!"

Mortimer turns. He hadn't seen the porcupine come out from behind the tree again. He knows he needn't be afraid. Porcupines don't eat mice, but they are much BIGGER than your average mouse.

Mortimer turns to face the porcupine, but shuffles slowly backward toward the tall grass, just in case.

"Hello. What can I do for you Mister Porcupine?" Asks Mortimer.

"Allow me to introduce myself," the porcupine says as he bows. "My name is Parker Porcupine. I must apologize for shouting just now, but I was wondering if you could assist me?"

Mortimer is amazed that Parker' quills remain flat even as he bows, his nose nearly touching the ground. That is a neat trick. He is obviously trying to appear as friendly as possible. Mortimer stops shuffling.

Since Mortimer has already noticed that something is bothering Parker, he decides to see what he can do to help. Although he isn't sure exactly how a mouse could possibly help a porcupine.

Mortimer bows too, letting his long tail do a big curl at the end. "Hello Parker, my name is Mortimer Mouse. I don't know how a mouse can help a porcupine, but I do have some time this morning. What is the matter?"

"I've lost it," Parker says.

"Lost what?"

"My curiosity. It's gone."

"Oh, I'm sorry. I've never seen one of those before. I don't think I can help you," admits a relieved Mortimer as he turns to continue on his way.

"What?" Parker gasps.

Mortimer looks back over his shoulder. "How can I help you find something if I don't even know what it is? That's a bit silly don't you think? I do hope you find it soon! Have a good day." Mortimer swivels his head around to continue on his way.

Parker starts laughing, quills sticking up in every direction, the ends quivering as he holds on to his middle trying not to fall over. "Oh, thank you, good friend. You have helped me already!"

Mortimer turns around once again to face Parker, wondering if he is just a little bit crazy. He doesn't think he's said anything funny. Mortimer waits patiently while Parker gradually calms down, quills arranging themselves to lie flat once again down his back.

Still chuckling a little to himself, Parker tries to explain. "Curiosity isn't like a ball or a deck of cards or even a building or a car. It doesn't have a color or a shape or a smell or a sound."

"Then how do you know that you lost it if you can't see it in the first place?" Mortimer twitches his whiskers. He is now pretty sure that Parker is crazy. And the only thing that might be worse than an unhappy porcupine is a crazy porcupine. A smart mouse knows when to run. Mortimer gets ready to skedaddle.

Parker can see that Mortimer wants to escape. "Please, wait. Please. I truly appreciate your helping me laugh. I am not laughing at you. I forgot that curiosity for a mouse is like water for a fish, which makes you the ideal person to help me if you would."

Mortimer snorts and thinks to himself, "Fish? You are making absolutely no sense. What do fish have to do with this?" He flicks his tail three times in annoyance. Really. If this goes on much longer, he will have to skip his quiet time altogether. That will not be a good start to the day.

Something keeps Mortimer rooted to the spot. He can't seem to leave. He has to see if he can help Parker solve this puzzle. Otherwise, he will wonder and wonder and wonder about it. Plus, he had been wondering about something else before he even saw the porcupine. He still needs to think about that, too! What was it? Oh, yes. Do rivers stop and think?

Mortimer brings his attention back to Mister Parker Porcupine, who, it turns out, is staring at him intently. "What were you doing just now?"

"What do you mean, what was I doing?" Asks Mortimer.

"You flicked your tail three times like you were annoyed, then your eyes got this far away look in them."

"Oh, I was wondering about your puzzle and this question I was thinking about as I walked here."

"Ah, I see. What was the question?

The visitor stands up and circles behind the tree. Now Mortimer can see the quills sticking up in all directions from the creature's back. "A porcupine! Fascinating, indeed! I wonder why he is here pacing around the tree?"

The porcupine emerges from behind the tree and sighs. He stands up on his hind legs and sniffs the air, his quills reaching out in every direction. After a moment, he plops back down on all fours, quills collapsing, and smells the ground. Then he proceeds to go around the tree again, this time in the opposite direction.

Mortimer sighs, too. "Not only have I found a porcupine, but he doesn't seem to be a very happy porcupine. Perhaps I shall have to find another place to sit and think today. One can hardly sit and think while an upset porcupine is pacing about."

Mortimer decides to continue past the tree along the river to search for another thinking spot. He is almost to the tall grass on the other side of the clearing when a deep voice rumbles, "Hey, you there, little mouse!"

the tall oak tree.

Mortimer stands on his hind legs and sniffs the air, whiskers twitching. He doesn't recognize the stranger by his smell, though.

"Well, I shouldn't be surprised that someone else is here," Mortimer says to himself. "This is an excellent thinking spot. Just the kind of place to stop and wonder about life, the world, and everything. Perhaps we shall have to keep an appointment book in a box to avoid interruptions."

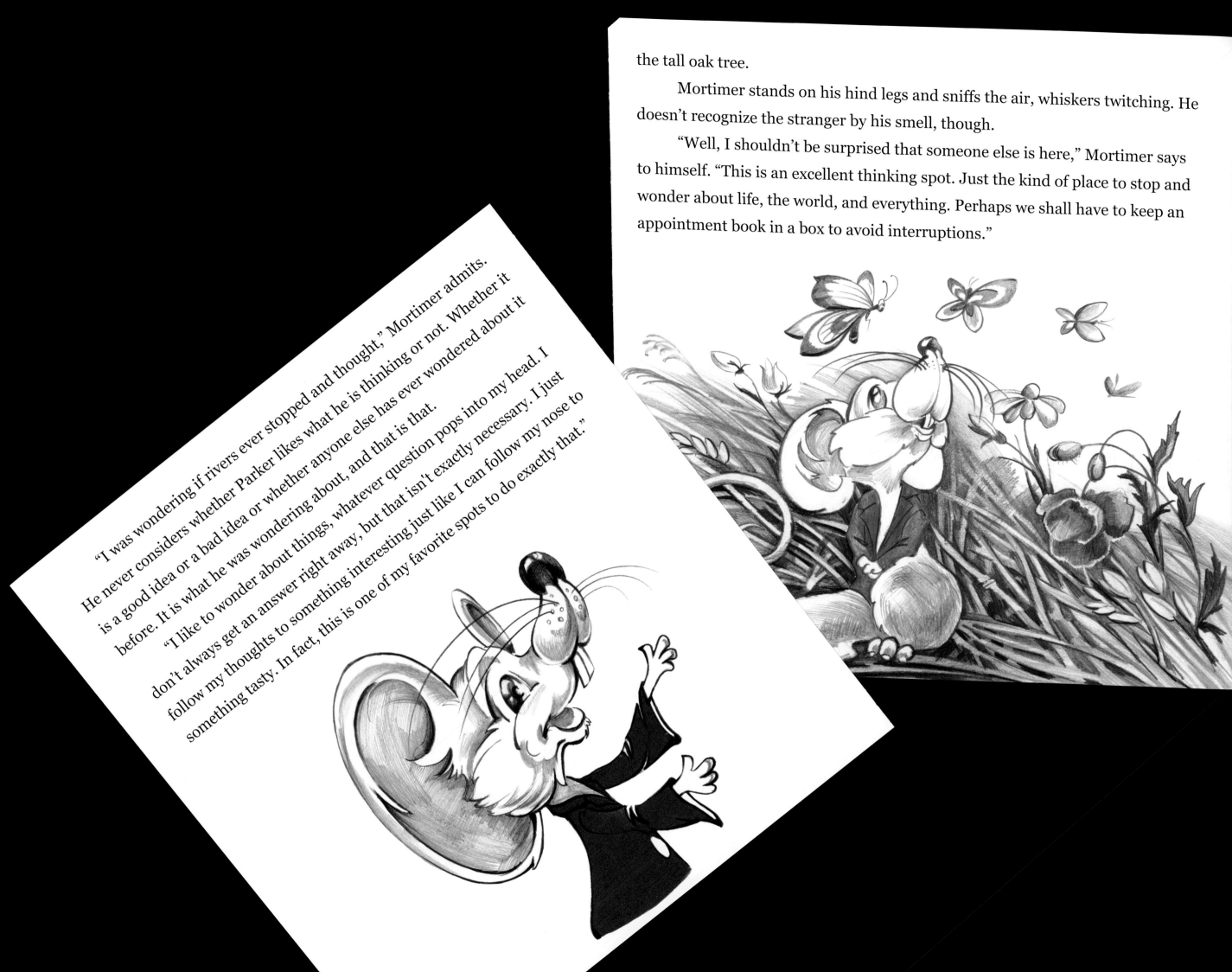

"I was wondering if rivers ever stopped and thought," Mortimer admits. He never considers whether Parker likes what he is thinking or not. Whether it is a good idea or a bad idea or whether anyone else has ever wondered about it before. It is what he was wondering about, and that is that.

"I like to wonder about things, whatever question pops into my head. I don't always get an answer right away, but that isn't exactly necessary. I just follow my thoughts to something interesting just like I can follow my nose to something tasty. In fact, this is one of my favorite spots to do exactly that."

"You, my friend, have just described curiosity perfectly. It always starts with a question, whether or not we ask it out loud." Parker chuckles one more time as he settles back against the old oak tree. "See, I told you. Your curiosity is as natural as breathing or as you described, as natural as smelling. I haven't been curious about anything in a long time."

"Are you sure about that?" Mortimer thinks he might be able to help after all.

"Oh, yes. I am quite sure. I get up in the morning. I go searching for something to eat. I talk with my friends, then I go to sleep and start all over again."

It is Mortimer's turn to laugh. "But you just asked me a question."

"A question? What do you mean?"

"You just asked me what I was doing. You wanted to know what I was thinking," says Mortimer.

Parker pauses for a second. "Yes, yes I did. It looked like you were thinking something interesting."

"You were CURIOUS. Weren't you?"

"Ha!" Parker shakes his head. "You are correct Mortimer. I WAS curious about what you were thinking. And I was right; you were thinking something interesting. I must say that you were right that this is an excellent wondering spot."

Mortimer claps his hands. "Let's wonder together! I bet if we sit and wonder about whether a river stops to think, we will find even more things to wonder about."

Mortimer
Mouse scrambles
up the oak tree and along
his favorite branch over the
river. Parker Porcupine climbs up
and sits next to his new friend. Mortimer
and Parker spend the morning together on the
tree branch talking and wondering about the river

. . . and many other things.